William Hooper

Fifty Years Since

Anatiposi

William Hooper

Fifty Years Since

Reprint of the original, first published in 1859.

1st Edition 2023 | ISBN: 978-3-38231-206-0

Anatiposi Verlag is an imprint of Outlook Verlagsgesellschaft mbH.

Verlag (Publisher): Outlook Verlag GmbH, Zeilweg 44, 60439 Frankfurt, Deutschland
Vertretungsberechtigt (Authorized to represent): E. Roepke, Zeilweg 44, 60439 Frankfurt, Deutschland
Druck (Print): Books on Demand GmbH, In de Tarpen 42, 22848 Norderstedt, Deutschland

FIFTY YEARS SINCE:

AN ADDRESS,

DELIVERED BEFORE THE ALUMNI OF THE UNIVERSITY OF
NORTH-CAROLINA,

ON THE 7TH OF JUNE, 1859,

(Being the day before the Annual Commencement.)

BY

WILLIAM HOOPER,

ONE OF THE SOCIETY OF ALUMNI.

Forsan et hæc olim meminisse juvabit.
VIRG.

———— Think oft, ye brethren——
Think of the gladness of our youthful prime;
It cometh not again—that golden time.
MOTTO TO STUDENT LIFE IN GERMANY.

Published by Order of the Society.

RALEIGH:
HOLDEN & WILSON, "STANDARD" OFFICE.
1859.

PREFACE.

~~~~~~~~~~~~~~

Those who heard the following Address delivered, will recollect, that owing to want of time, much of it was not read. They will, therefore, not be surprised to find here much that they did not hear. The author could not wish for his essay a happier fate than that it should receive from the reading public the same approbation that was accorded to it by a most good-natured audience, rendered so by the exhilarating presence of the President of the United States.

June, 1859

ADDRESS
BEFORE THE ALUMNI OF THE UNIVERSITY
OF
NORTH-CAROLINA.

BROTHERS OF THE ALUMNI—
    LITERARY CHILDREN OF ONE ALMA MATER:

WE come together at this annual festival, to salute and congratulate each other—to look back on the past and compare it with the present—to gratify an honest pride in contrasting the feeble and sickly infancy of our literary mother with her present vigorous maturity, and to breathe a common filial prayer that that vigorous maturity may long flourish, and not soon be succeeded by a languishing old age.

Two years ago, I delivered, at another College, what I expected would be my final offering at the shrine of the muses: but since the committee, representing the public opinion, have not consented to give me a discharge from this mode of paying a debt of filial gratitude, I submit to their dictation, being glad to receive, in such appointment, their flattering attestation that they yet detect no mark of senility disqualifying me for appearing before a commencement audience, and especially the audience of 1859, so highly honored by the presence of the chief magistrate of the republic. I am proud to find, from two astronomical observations, that Chapel Hill lies right in the orbit of Jupiter and his satellites, and that the period of his revolution is about twelve years. I beg the professor of astronomy here to make this entry in his *Ephemeris*, and to look out for the recurrence of the same phenomenon about 1871; if indeed, at that time, the head of this great republic be fitly symbolized by that glorious planet, and be not shivered, ere that cycle rolls around, by some disastrous concussion, into a score of nameless asteroids. May heaven avert the omen! Had I said this at the city of Washington, and were I some quarter of a century younger, his Excellency might consider this exordium as the prelude to some application for office; but on an academical jubilee like this, and from a speaker bordering on three-score and seven, he will receive it, I trust, only as the cordial and sincere expression of that rejoicing which we all feel at the honor of this visit. Yes, a truce from office-seeking here at least. We are glad to find that the President has survived that period of vexatious importunity—that crown of thorns which every President is obliged to wear on his first accession,—and that he is likely, from present appearances, to serve his country for many years to come.

I believe it is expected of the speaker to the Alumni that he shall entertain them with reminiscences of persons and things long gone by—the longer the better. Hence the selection, for this year, of your humble servant, there being very few now surviving who can number half a century from their graduation. And although I am neither a bachelor nor a widower, and therefore have no interest in making myself out younger than I am with my fair auditors, yet I will merely hint to this benevolent assembly that although it is just fifty years since I got my sheepskin, I was then in my *prætexta,* and had not yet put on the *toga virilis.* I shall, however, be happy if I get through the task of this day without extorting from some of my hearers the exclamation of the Roman satirist: "The old steed is broken down; take him from the turf before he disgraces himself." *

Particularly might my friends be anxious about me now as having to perform my part of the duties of this occasion after the display of this morning. I assure them that I feel a great degree of tranquility in that very consideration which they might deem a just cause of agitation and disquietude, to-wit:

---

* Solve senescentem mature sanus equum ne
Peccet ad extremum, ridendus.—Hor.

That I am succeeding *the orator of the day.* · " I am no orator
as Brutus is." Upon him I roll the responsibility of supply-
ing all the eloquence due to the day. His shoulders are well
able to bear the burden ; while to me remains only the easier
part of the master of ceremonies, to announce to the audience
" Ladies and gentlemen! the concert is over." *

When I look back through the vista of those fifty years and
bring before my " mind's eye " the long train of alumni who
have risen to eminence and adorn their country, both at
home and abroad, I may be indulged in something of a spirit
of glorying, if as a professor of the University, I have had
any share in the formation of these ornaments of the republic.
I confess, when I look over the catalogue of graduates, and
see so many laureled heads into which it was my lot to pack
a portion of useful knowledge, I am elated with a little of
that pride which swelled the breast of the mother of the gods
on Mount Olympus, as she looked at her children around
her :

> See all her progeny, illustrious sight!
> Behold and count them, as they rise to light ;
> She sees around her in the blest abode,
> A hundred sons, and every son a god!

I have said that it is perhaps expected of the alumni address, that it shall entertain you with reminiscences ; and I
hope I shall not be too severely judged, if in preparing this
entertainment, I looked forward to a hot day, a crowded
house, and a great deal of grave business,—all which anticipations warranted me in the selection of reminiscences of an
amusing, as well as of an instructive kind. Indeed, a retrospect of Chapel Hill antiquities, so far back as half-a-century,
must needs bring up many a scene of so comic a nature.

> That to be grave, exceeds all power of face.
> In telling or in hearing of the case.

* This paragraph was added after hearing the splendid speech of Mr. McRae in the
forenoon.

The first of the Waverly novels was entitled " Sixty Years Since," which serves as a date to the origin of those wonderful compositions. My tale shall be entitled " Fifty Years Since," though some of my story will embrace incidents within forty years of the present date ; and if it fall (as of course it will) infinitely below that of the renowned Sir Walter, in all other respects, it will rise above him in one; that whereas most of his is fiction, mine is sober fact. At least, I intend it to be so. But it may be with me as it was with Boswell, in his celebrated " Life of Dr. Johnson." He tells us that it was his habit, after being in company with his hero, to go immediately to his lodgings and record the sayings and doings of the Dr., at once, while they were fresh in his memory; but that sometimes, when circumstances interfered, the facts lay on his memory for a day or two, and that he thought *they were the better of it—as they had a chance to grow mellow !*

I hope that if any of my co-evals are present, who can look back as far into our antiquities as myself, they will not have occasion to say, when they hear some of my recitals : " There is a fact that has grown *mellow* in his memory," or to compare me with the aged harper in Scott's Lay of the Last Minstrel :

> " Each blank in faithless memory void,
> The poet's glowing thought supplied."

It is my part then, to-day, to go back to the very *increnabula* of our college, —the cradle of its infancy, and to call up recollections of some who rocked that cradle. And I dare say while I am telling the story of the poor and beggarly minority of our *alma mater*, some of her proud, saucy sons of the present generation will smile scornfully at the humility of our origin. When I tell them that the classes of President Polk,—of Governors Branch, Brown, Manly, Morehead, Mosely, Spaight—of Judges Murphy, Cameron, Martin, Donnell, Williams, Mason, Anderson ; of Senators Mangum and Haywood—of Drs. Hawks, Morrison, Green, and of many other graduates forty years back, eminent for merit though not holding office—when I tell the proud collegians of the present day, that these men came out of classes consisting of nine, ten, fourteen, fifteen, the largest twenty-one,—they will set up a broad laugh, and think how poor a figure a class of ten or fifteen must cut on a commencement day: and one will say: "Why I graduated with *seventy-five*," and another: "I with one hundred," and another: "I with a hundred and ten." Well, I know of no better way to shelter myself from the storm of your ridicule, than by telling you a story. "Once upon a time," says Æsop, "a fox brought out her whole brood of little foxes, and paraded them before the lioness, and said: 'Look here! see what a family I have, whereas you have but one!' 'I know said the queen of beasts that I bear but one at a time, but then he is a lion!'" I would also remind you, young classics, of the story of Niobe, who boasted of her twelve children, and crowed over Latona, who had only two; but then Latona's children were the sun and moon! Forgive, young gentlemen, these boastings of an old man. You know it is the characteristic of such a one, to overrate the past, and underrate the present. But I trust I am sufficiently sensible of the vast advances made in all things at Chapel Hill since my day, to do full justice to the present age. You have turned the wild into a garden. You have substituted for the meagre bill of fare with which our minds were obliged to content themselves, a table rich in all the stores of learning which a half-century of unexampled progress has heaped upon it. I hope therefore, when I roll back the volume of our college history, and show you "the day of small things," you will not despise too much our petty number, our humble accommodations, our rude manners, our hard fare, our scanty rations, and our limited *curriculum* of studies. Let not

> Grandeur hear with a disdainful smile,
> The short and simple annals of the poor.

When I first knew Chapel Hill in January, 1804, the infant university was but about six years old. Its only finished buildings were what are now called the East Wing and the Old Chapel. The former was then only two stories high, capable of accomodating one tutor and sixty students by crowding four into a room. The faculty consisted of three : President Caldwell, Prof. Bingham, and tutor Henderson. Their college titles were "Old Joe," "Old Slick" and "Little Dick." "Old Joe," however, was only thirty years of age, and possessed (as you shall hear in the sequel) a formidable share of youthful activity. "Old Slick" derived his cognomen, not from age, but from premature baldness, and the extreme glossiness of his naked scalp. And "Little Dick," a cousin of the late distinguished Judge Henderson, though he had a brave spirit, was not very well fitted by the size of his person, to overawe the three score rude chaps over whom he was placed as solitary sentinel. As a nursery of the college there was then a preparatory school, taught by Matthew Troy and Chesley Daniel. All things were fashioned after the model of Princeton college, and that probably was fashioned after the model of the Scottish universities, by old Dr. Witherspoon. If this were the case, it would seem to account for the small quantum of instruction provided for us. if Dr. Johnson spoke the truth when he said of Scottish education, that "there, every body got a mouthful, but nobody got a belly-full." Into this preparatory school, it was my fortune to be inducted, a trembling urchin of twelve years, in the winter of 1804. It was then a barbarous custom brought from the North, to rise at that severe season of the year, before day-light and to go to prayers by candle-light; and many a cold wintry morning do I recollect, trudging along in the dark at the heels of Mr., afterwards Dr. Caldwell, with whom I boarded, on our way to the tutor's room, to wait for the second bell. In that year I read Sallust's War of Jugurtha and Conspiracy of Catiline, under the tuition of Mr. Troy, of whom my recollections are affectionate, for he was partial to me, and taught me well for those times. But I can recollect some of my classmates, grown young men, upon whose backs he tried a blister-plaster, made of chinque-pin bark, to quicken the torpor of the brain. Nor was he

singular in his discipline. Whether boys were then duller or
more idle than now, I know not, but at that time whipping
was the order of the day. I had, before coming to Chapel
Hill, served three years under it, at Hillsboro', where Mr.
Flinn wielded his terrible sceptre, and realized in our eye,
the description of Goldsmith :

> " A man severe he was and stern to view ;
> I knew him well, and every truant knew ;
> Well had the boding tremblers learned to trace
> The day's disasters in his morning face."

This was literally verified with us, when Dr. Flinn came to
school on Monday morning, with his head tied with a crim-
son bandana handkerchief. It was the bloody flag to us, and
the very skin of our backs began to tremble.

After serving such an apprenticeship at Hillsboro', the ex-
change for Mr. Troy's administration was like exchanging
the cowhide for the willow twig, for Mr. Flinn's "little
finger was thicker than Mr. Troy's loins." But now after
drawing aside the pall of oblivion from these infirmities of
the dead, I feel some twinges of remorse, as though I had
rudely trodden on the ashes of my departed instructors ; for,
having been myself a teacher, all my life, I ought to know
how to make allowance for the trials of teachers ; and if any
one of you, my hearers, is accustomed to rail at the tyranny
of pedagogues, and to flatter yourself with the conceit, that
if you were one, you would always be able to control your
temper, I would only address you in the language which the
advertisement uses respecting sovereign recipes : "Try it,"
and if in six months you don't go and hang yourself, you
will, at least, have more charity for teachers, all the days of
your life. I told you that I remembered Mr. Troy with gratitude ; but I believe nothing he ever taught me, imprinted
itself so deeply on my memory, as the burst of eloquence
which the boys told me he had made, when he was a student,
upon the charms of Miss Hay, afterwards the first Mrs. Gaston. Troy was given to the grandiloquent style, and on this

occasion Miss Hay, who was the belle of the day, with a small party came to visit the Dialectic library. It was then kept in one of the common rooms inhabited by four students; and you may judge of the tumult that was excited by every such visitation, and how much sweeping and fixing up was required, and how many frightened boys ran to the neighboring rooms, and shut the doors, all but a small crack to peep through. On this memorable occasion, Troy had fixed himself in a corner of the room, whence he could contemplate the beautiful apparition in silent ecstasy. After she was gone, the librarian called him out of his trance, and said: " Well, Troy, what do you think of her ?" "Oh! sir, she's enough to melt the frigidity of a stoic, and excite rapture in the breast of a hermit;" to which he might have added :

" And like another Helen, has fired another Troy."

A man that could talk in that way, appeared to me, in those days, to have reached the top of Parnassus.

Having mentioned the library of one of the literary societies, I must carry you back, ye proud Dialectics and Philanthropics of the present age, to your humble birth, and reveal to you your inglorious antecedents. It may be good for you who now loll upon sofas and survey with triumph your thousands of volumes to look back fifty-five years, and glance your eye "into the hole of the pit whence ye were digged." The Dialectic library of this college, all of it, was then contained in one of the cupboards of one of the common rooms in the east building, and consisted of a few half-worn volumes, presented by compassionate individuals, and I think it was in the habit of migrating from room to room, as the librarian was changed, for you may be sure the responsibility of taking care of such a number of books could not be borne long by one pair of shoulders. And besides, there was some ambition to choose, as librarian, a man who could wait on the ladies with something of that courtly grace which distinguishes the marshals of this polished age. But the cavaliers of that early time, poor fellows! had to make their way to the ladies' hearts without any of the modern artillery of splendid sashes, moustaches and goatees. The naked face, with native flush or native pallor, was all their dependance. The cupboards were not only small but full of rat-holes, and a large rat might have taken his seat upon Rollins' History, the corner stone of the library, and exclaimed with Robinson Crusoe:

> " I am monarch of all I survey,
> My title there's none to dispute."

Such was the infancy of Dialectic knowledge; such the meagre fare provided for Dialectic literary appetite in those primeval days.

And what is told of one library may be told of the other, for they were as much alike as the teeth of the upper and the lower jaw, and as often came into collision. When one library got a book, the other must have the same book, only more handsomely bound, if possible. I am sorry to record that the contest between the two societies, at that time, was not confined to an honorable competition which should have the finest library, or the best scholars; but that it often amounted to personal rancor and sometimes seemed to threaten a general battle.

The societies then had no halls of their own, but held their sessions on different nights in the week in the old chapel, without any fire in the winter, and besides, with the north-wind pouring in through many a broken pane. Think of this, ye pampered collegians, of this effeminate age, and bless your stars that your college times have come fifty years later.

Before I come down to a somewhat later period, let me present you with a sketch of the scenes going on under these old oaks in the year 1804, fifty-five years ago, and let me draw from memory, if I can, a picture of the 4th of July of that year, for that was the commencement day—the great national festival being then the great college festival.

The waves of the revolutionary war seemed hardly to have subsided, and hence military feeling and military habits intruded upon academic shades and mixed themselves with the

peaceful pursuits of literature. The great object of display
on commencement day was not the graduates or their
speeches, but a fourth of July oration, delivered by the
General, who had been chosen by the vote of the whole body
of students, preps and all, for free suffrage then prevailed,
and a preps vote was as good as any body's. The office of
General and orator of the day was, of course, an object of
great ambition; and while the election was pending, we
preps felt our importance considerably augmented. Like the
Nile, we always began to swell about the end of June; but
our inundation was sooner over, not lasting longer than the
fourth of July. On these occasions the candidates would
come down among us and take us in their arms and caress
us most lovingly, and invite us to their rooms in college, and,
I suppose, treat us there to gingercakes and cider, though as
to that fact, I have no distinct recollection; but all of you who
are versed in the ways of candidates, will admit it to be very
probable that they did. As well as I recollect, there was
elected, beside the General or orator, the General's aid. On
this occasion Thomas Brown, son of the late Gen. Brown, of
Bladen, and brother-in-law of the late Gov. Owen, was
elected General, and Hyder Ally Davie, son of Gen. Davie,
was second in command.

All things being duly arranged, the General, clad in full
regimentals, with cocked hat and dancing red plume, placed
himself at the head of his troops (for we were all turned into
soldiers, for the nonce) and marched up to the foot of the
"Big Poplar," where was placed for him a rostrum, upon
which he mounted, and, all the military disposing themselves
before him, he gracefully took off his plumed helmet, and
made profound obeisance to the army; and if a prep's bosom
ever throbbed with proud emotions and ever thrilled with
anticipations of the pleasure of being a great man, our hearts
felt that throb and that thrill on that day. I can tell you
nothing of the graduating class, or their speeches. My child-
ish fancy was taken up with the military display, though we
had no music to march to but the drum and fife. If we had

had such a band as you have here to-day, it might have been too much for us—few perhaps would have survived it.

The ball at night was productive of an incident of some seriousness and importance. The old Steward's Hall, which some of you have reason still to recollect to your sorrow, was then the ball-room. The floor was covered with spectators, except the spots left vacant for the dancers. Of course the dancers had to pull their partners to their position through a dense thicket of gentlemen, five deep. This may well be called "threading one's way," I should think. In such circumstances dancing in the month of July, must have been delectable work, and must have always involved the risk of such unhappy rencounters as the one I am about to describe. Hyder Davie, aid-de-camp to Gen. Brown, in cutting the pigeon-wing before his partner, came down, rough-shod, upon the toes of Henry Chambers, of Salisbury. It was borne with, the first time, as an accident and overlooked; but upon coming round the second time, it was repeated, and consequently was obliged to be considered as an intended insult. The wounded toe, which is sometimes the seat of honor, called the offending heel out of doors, and demanded an explanation. It resulted in an engagement, in which Chambers gave a blow or two, for which he received a stab or two, in the neck, from the pen-knife of Davie; for in those simple days bowie-knives were not invented, nor arms worn, except openly by soldiers. The next day a solemn trial of the case was held in the chapel, by the trustees, among whom were Gen. Davie, Col. Polk, (chairman,) Gov. Martin, Messrs. Cameron, Gaston, Nash and others, since the men of mark in our State. What decision the trustees came to, is not recollected, but I believe the combatants came off even. The ladies, the next day, were found to have taken sides, some for the heel and some for the toe, like the Little-Endians and Big-Endians, familiar to the readers of Gulliver.

I will detain you on this part of my subject only a moment, to call your attention to two things characteristic of the age. The first is, the spirit of the times indicated by the name Hyder Ally, given to *his* son, by Gen. Davie, and that of

Tippoo Saib, given to *his* son by Maj. Pleasant Henderson. That two such men should have given their sons such out-landish names, in honor of two Hindoo despots and semi-barbarians, because they were at war with Great Britain, affords a lively idea of the old flame against the mother country, still burning in the breasts of the surviving officers of the revolution.

The second reflection suggested by the incident before us, is the diminutive size of the ladies of those days. How un-ambitious, how feeble-minded they must have been to be contented with occupying no more space in the world, and in the eyes of men, to be pulled, that way, through a zig-zag maze of rough arms and shoulders, at the imminent risk of hanging by the hair or losing a comb or necklace in the transit. The ladies of the present day, have learned too well their just rights, to be satisfied with anything less than *two-thirds* of this wide, wide world. There is no limit to their inventive genius when it is stimulated by an encroachment on their rightful domains. They have added to the dimen-sions of their fame, as well as of their persons, by giving birth to a new order of architecture. A modern fine lady is, herself, a novel and wondrous specimen of architecture. Look at those two delicate little ankles! From the time of the erection of the Parthenon—from the time of the erection of the domes of St. Peter's and St. Paul's, down to the erec-tion of the domes at Washington or Raleigh, was it ever supposed—would it ever have been believed—did it ever enter into the heads of Phidias, Michael Angelo, or Sir Christopher Wren, that two such slender columns would have supported so stupendous a dome—especially columns con-structed on the most unartistic of all principles, the inverted cone? It can be classed with no order of architecture now extant. We shall have to invent a new name for it, and I can think of none more appropriate than the Umbrella Order of Architecture. They who have dared to prop up such a magnificent fabric upon such a pedestal, have found out the *pou sto* of Archimedes, and can move the universe.

It was at this commencement, I think (1804) that Greek

was made a part of the college course. Gov. Martin, if I recollect, was the proposer of the measure. "You study logic," said he, "and you don't know the word from which the term is derived." No doubt the Governor gave some better arguments (if I had been old enough to cherish them) for substituting the classics of Greece for those of France, which last had then a factitious importance and popularity from the recent splendor of Voltaire, from our late obligations to the country of La Fayette, and from the overwhelming interest excited by the first French revolution. A little French had, before this time, been accepted in the place of Greek, and a Frenchman had been a necessary "part and parcel" of the faculty. Of course, to torment him, and amuse themselves with his transports of rage, and his broken English, was a regular part of the college fun. The trustees after some experience found that it was better to have French taught by a competent American, though with a little less of the Parisian accent, than to have to fight daily battles to redress the grievances of a persecuted monsieur. Greek, after its introduction, became the bug-bear of college. Having been absent when my class began it, I heard, on my return, such a terrific account of it, that I no more durst encounter the Greeks than Xerxes when he fled in consternation across the Hellespont, after the battle of Salamis. Rather than lose my degree, however, after two years, I plucked up courage, and set doggedly and desperately to work, prepared hastily thirty Dialogues of Lucian, and on that stock of Greek was permitted to graduate. As for Chemistry and Differential and Integral Calculus and all that, we never heard of such hard things. They had not then crossed the Roanoke, nor did they appear among us, till they were brought in by the northern barbarians, about the year 1818. Yet notwithstanding the poor showing we could make as to faculty and course of study, the secretary of the board of that day, was very ambitious of opening a sisterly correspondence and communion with all the colleges of the United States. He sent for all their Latin Catalogues, and in order to be even with them, made up, out of his own stock of Latin, a Cata-

2

logue for us, and diffused it through the land, from Maine to Georgia. Now this was very unwise policy in that officer, for we were then in the very egg-shell of our existence, and ought to have concealed our nakedness from our mocking brethren of the North. This Latin pamphlet was, in every respect, a sorry looking affair. It was gotten up at Raleigh, on coarse paper, and it can be no offence now to say, that Raleigh was not at that era a fortunate place of issue for a Latin pamphlet. But what was worse, it was disfigured with several sad blunders in the Latin (for I don't know that Latin is any part of the qualifications of a secretary of the board) and exhibited to the admiring world the following imposing *Senatus Academicus:* PRESIDENT CALDWELL, who taught mathematics, natural and moral philosophy, and did all the preaching. YOUR HUMBLE SERVANT was professor of languages, in general, I suppose; all, ancient and modern; and WILLIAM D. MOSELEY (the future governor of Florida) was tutor. The professor of languages was of course responsible for this elegant and classical production, in which, among other beauties, I recollect the treasurers of the board were called in conspicuous capitals TREASURARII! I writhed under the mortification a long time, and was always afraid of meeting a professor from the North, lest he should ask me what was the Latin for *treasurer*.

The South building, our neighbor over there, was then in an unfinished state, carried up a story and a half, and there left for many years to battle with the weather unsheltered; but still it was inhabited. "Inhabited!" you will say, "by what? By toads and snails and bats, I suppose." No sir, by students. *Risum teneatis amici?*

As the only dormitory that had a roof was too crowded for study, and as those who tried to study there spent half the evening in passing laws to regulate the other half, many students left their rooms as a place of study entirely, and built cabins in the corners of the unfinished brick walls, and quite comfortable cabins they were; but whence the plank came, out of which those cabins were built, your deponent saith not. Suffice it to hint that in such matters college boys

are apt to adopt the code of Lycurgus: that there is no harm
in privately transfering property, provided you are not caught
at it. In such a cabin your speaker and dozens like him
hibernated and burned their midnight oil. As soon as spring
brought back the swallows and the leaves, we emerged from
our dens and chose some shady retirement where we made a
path and a promenade, and in that embowered promenade
all diligent students of those days had to follow the steps of
science, to wrestle with its difficulties, and to treasure up their
best acquirements :

> Ye remnants of the *Peripatetic* school!
> Ah! ye can tell how hard it is to climb
> The steep where fame's proud temple shines afar!

They lived *sub dio*, like the birds that caroled over their
heads. "But how," you will say, "did they manage in rainy
weather?" Aye, that's the rub. Well, nothing was more
common than, on a rainy day, to send in a petition to be ex-
cused from recitation, which petition ran in this stereotype
phrase: "The inclemency of the weather rendering it impos-
sible to prepare the recitation, the Sophomore class respectfully
request Mr. Rhea to excuse them from recitation this after-
noon." To deliver this mission to the Professor I was appoint-
ed envoy ordinary (not extraordinary) and plenipotentiary,
being a little fellow hardly fifteen, and perhaps somewhat of
a pet with the teacher. The Professor, a good-natured, indo-
lent man, after affecting some vexation, (though he was
secretly glad to get off himself,) and pushing the end of his
long nose this way and that way some half a dozen times
with his knuckles, concluded in a gruff voice with: "Well,
get as much more for to-morrow." The shout of applause
with which I was greeted upon reporting the success of my
embassy resembled, (if we may compare small things with
great,) the acclamations with which Mr. Webster was hailed
by the nation upon happily concluding the Ashburton treaty
in 1842, by which war with Great Britain was prevented.
Mr. Webster may have been greater, but he was not prouder

than I was at the successful issue of my negotiations. Who knows but I might now have been a first rate diplomate, if I had followed up these auspicious beginnings! And what do you think was the *lesson* from which a deliverance for one day was the occasion of such tumultuous joy? Why, it was *Morse's geography*, which was then the main Sophomore study, contained in two massy octavos, and to recite off which, like a speech, page by page, was the test and the glory of the first scholar of the class.

Dr. Morse was, with us, the great man of the age, and stood as high as does now his son, the inventor of the telegraph : and that notwithstanding he had stigmatised our State by mentioning under the head of "manns and customers of North-Carolina," that a fashionable amusement of our people in their personal rencounters was, for the combatant who got his antagonist down to insert his thumb into the corner of his eye and twist out the ball; which elegant operation they called *gouging*. This slur upon our national character would, now-a-days, have banished his book from the State. It excited so much the wrath of one of our representatives in Congress, Wm. Barry Grove, of Fayetteville, that he declared if he ever met with Dr. Morse he would gouge him. He *did* meet with the Doctor, who had heard of the threat, but instead of executing his purpose they had a hearty laugh over the story, Dr. Morse alleging that he had derived the account from Williamson.

Our geographical recitations were enlivened by some rare scenes, one or two of which I will venture to relate, though they are almost too farcical for this dignified assembly, and yet they are among the things, "as my Lord Verulam remarks, which men do not willingly let die." The class was reciting on *Greenland*. The youth under examination was ―― ――, I do not feel safe to mention his name, for he may be here among us for aught I know, (*the speaker looking anxiously over the crowd*,) but if he is, he will be easily known by the length of his ears, and there are no animals on earth that bite and kick harder than the long-eared tribe. We will, therefore, indicate him by the name *Sawney*. Mr. Sawney, says the Professor, can you tell me anything about the animals of Greenland? "Yes, sir, there's one called the seal." What kind of an animal is it? "I don't remember exactly, sir, but I believe he says it is a very amphib— a *very amphibiobus* kind of animal, sir." The boys plagued him about this new kind of animal until he became as irritable as a nest of wasps by the way-side. Another student, whom we will disguise under the name of *Riggie*, used to amuse various companies by telling the story upon Sawney. Now Riggie was the last man that ought to have made people merry over the blunders of others, for he had got his own nickname by his ludicrous pronunciation of *Riga*, a Russian town on the Baltic. He was asked what were the chief towns in Russia? He mentioned several, and among them *Riggie* on the *Baltic*, pronouncing the first syllable of the last word as it is heard in *balance*. The name Riggie stuck to him forever afterwards. But it often happens that he who smarts most under a joke is most ready to avert pursuit by throwing ridicule upon others—as in the street, the thief, hearing the hue and cry after him, escapes by echoing the cry "*stop thief!*" and joining in the chase. Sawney, goaded by Riggie's persecution, determined to avenge himself; so he laid a trap for him. He got a friend to invite a company including Riggie into his room, and to call for the story, while in the meantime, Sawney concealed himself under the bed. Riggie, alas! unconscious of the Trojan horse within the walls, was going on with his story, full sail, the audience convulsed with the enjoyment of the present and the anticipation of the paulo-post-future; when in the very fifth act of the drama, out popped Sawney from his ambush, and pitched into the dismayed comedian. I shall not not attempt to describe the battle; but it may well be supposed that Sawney, stung with wounded pride and bursting with long imprisoned rage, fought with more desparation, and that his adversary, startled by a foe emerging suddenly from ambush, must have fought to a disadvantage. That was the last time I imagine that Riggie, or any body else, told the story of *amphibiobus*, nor would it have been revived to-day had I not trusted that a lapse of more than fifty years had either removed our hero from the reach of all earthly ridicule, or mollified his resentment into merriment; or at least, that being unnamed in my annals, he would take care not to write his name under the picture by attacking me. But if he or any other witness of the facts were here to challenge my truth and to show what a good story I had made out of nothing, I suppose you all would thank him about as much as you would thank a man, who, after you had dined pleasantly, as you supposed, upon a good fat hare, should come forward, show you the paws and convince you that what you had enjoyed so sweetly, was nothing but a *cat*.

Such adventures as the foregoing were more apt to happen with sophmores than with other classes. To save them from the clutches of Dr. Morse, on a rainy day, was one of the chief honors of my sophomore year. Sophomores have always been hard fellows to deal with. This results from their amphibious nature, and colleges have given them a name (*sophos moros*) expressive of their compound character, partly wise and partly foolish. They are in a transition state, half-man and half-boy; their voice alternating in a most ludicrous manner between the *alto* and the *bass*, so that, in the dark, you would suppose it was two persons talking. Their compositions too have the same mixed character; like comets they have a small nucleus with a prodigious expanse of tail.* Let not my young friends present, who happen to be sophomores, take umbrage at these pleasantries. I am not describing the sophomores of the present day, nor any specific sophomores. I am describing sophomores in the *abstract*, not in the concrete, and of course, no individual has a right to appropriate the description to himself, since the sophomore concrete has always specific peculiarities which shield him from being identified with the sophomore abstract. Besides, the glory of a sophomore is not in what he *is*, but in what he *is to be*. He is an eaglet. Now an eaglet, just beginning to

---

* In Webster's Dictionary, Mr. Calhoun's authority is given for the word *sophomor-ical* in this sense.

be fledged, may not be a very comely bird, and its attempts to fly may be rather awkward; but then in a month or two, he is to be the bird of Jove, soaring into the eye of the sun, and bearer of the thunderbolt.

JUNIOR LIFE.

Let me now give you a sketch of *junior* life, some fifty years ago in these precints. There being but three teachers in college, (president, professor of languages and tutor,) the seniors and juniors had but one recitation per day. The juniors had their first taste of geometry, in a little elementary treatise, drawn up by Dr. Caldwell, in manuscript, and not then printed. Copies were to be had only by transcribing, and in process of time, they, of course, were swarming with errors. But this was a decided advantage to the junior, who stuck to his text, without minding his diagram. For, if he happened to say the angle at A was equal to the angle at B, when, in fact the diagram showed no angle at B at all, but one at C, if Dr. Caldwell corrected him, he had it always in his power to say: "Well, that was what I thought myself, but it ain't so in the book, and I thought you knew better than I." We may well suppose that the Dr. was completely silenced by this unexpected application of the *argumentum ad hominem.* You see how good a training our youthful junior was under, by a faithful adherence to his text, to become a "strict constructionist" of the constitution, when he should ripen into a politician. The junior, having safely got through with his mathematical recitation at 11 o'clock, was free till the next day at the same hour. And the first thing he had to determine was, what would be the most agreeable method of spending the rest of the day. Shall he ramble into the country after fruit, or shall he go a fishing, or shall he make up a party and engage a supper in the suburbs, at "Fur Craigs?" The last measure was often adopted, because of our hard fare at Commons. Accordingly a party of some half-dozen would go out and engage a supper of fried chicken, or chicken pie, biscuit and coffee. It was waited for with extreme impatience, and many yawnings and other symptoms of an aching void. At length it came upon the table, like the classical *cœna* of the Romans, about three or four P. M. The guests sat down, at twenty-five cents per head ; and if you consider the leanness of our dinners at the Steward's Hall, you will be apt to suspect that the entertainer did not make much by that bargain. I'll tell you what, gentlemen, it will do well enough for you, who live in these palmy times, and fare sumptuously every day, to call the University your *alma mater*, your *benigna parens*, and all that, now that she is grown to be a fat, buxom lady, with a snug, dear income of fifteen thousand a year. But when I first knew her, she was a very poor woman, and her children of those days would have more appropriately called her "*pauperima mama!*" for she dealt out very scanty allowance to her family either for body or mind, and treated her sons as movers to our new States treat their horses ; she turned them out at night to pick up what they could. The truth is, *her* mother the State, acted a very unnatural part towards her, and, soon after she was born, seemed to take a dislike to her own off-spring, and to try to starve it. Do you wish to know the ordinary bill of fare at the Steward's Hall, fifty years ago ? As well as I recollect board per annum was thirty-five dollars ! This, as you may suppose, would not support a very luxurious table, but the first body of trustees were men who had seen the revolution, and they thought that sum would furnish as good rations as those lived on who won our liberties. Coarse corn bread was the staple food. At dinner the only meat was a fat middling of bacon, surmounting a pile of coleworts ; and the first thing after grace was said (and sometimes be-fore) was for one man, by a single horizontal sweep of his knife, to separate the ribs and lean from the fat, monopolize all the first to himself, and leave the remainder for his fel-lows. At breakfast we had wheat bread and butter and coffee. Our supper was coffee and the corn bread left at dinner, without butter. I remember the shouts of rejoicing when we had assembled at the door, and some one jumping up and looking in at the window, made proclamation : "Wheat bread for supper, boys!" And that wheat bread,

.er which such rejoicings were raised, believe me gentle-
nen and ladies, was manufactured out of wheat we call
seconds, or, as some term it, *grudgeons.* You will not wonder,
'' after such a supper, most of the students welcomed the
approach of night, as beasts of prey, that they might go a
prowling, and seize upon every thing eatable within the
compass of one or two miles; for, as I told you, our boys
were followers of the laws of Lycurgus. Nothing was secure
from the devouring torrent. Beehives, though guarded by a
thousand stings—all feathered tenants of the roost—water-
melon and potato patches, roasting ears, &c., in fine every
thing that could appease hunger, was found missing in the
morning. These marauding parties at night were often
wound up with setting the village to rights. I will relate
one of these nocturnal adventures, and it was only " *unum e
pluribus.*" I must premise that Dr. Caldwell seems to have
made it a part of his fixed policy, that no evil-doer should
hope to escape by the swiftness of heels, and that whoever
was surprised at night in any act of mischief, should be run
down, caught and brought to justice. Whether the Doctor
brought that feature of his policy from Princeton, where he
was educated, or whether, being conscious that nature had
gifted him with great nimbleness of foot, he was a little ambitious of victory in that line, I will not determine; but
certain it is, that he was in the habit of rambling about, at
night, in search of adventures, and whenever he came across
an unlucky wight engaged in taking off a gate, building a
fence across the street, driving a brother calf or goat into the
chapel, or any similar exploit of genius, he no sooner hove
in sight than he gave chase; nor did the youthful malefactor
spare his sinews that night; for he knew that if he ever ran
for life or glory, now was the time. Homer makes his hero
Achilles, the swiftest as well as the bravest on the plains of
Troy. No foe could match him in battle or escape him by
flight. Dr. Caldwell was the *podas okus Achilles* of Chapel
Hill, and he had more occasion for powers of pursuit than of
contest, for his antagonists uniformly took to flight. You call
this a " fast age," gentlemen, and so it is, but I don't know a

man of this generation who is faster than was Dr. Caldwell.
He liked to go fast in everything, and therefore he was not
satisfied to take two days in getting to Raleigh. He and I
have set out for the metropolis in the morning, and stopt the
first night at Pride's, ten miles this side, such was the state
of the roads. Who knows but such snail-like progress as
this suggested to him the first idea of the present railroad
from Beaufort to the mountains, the honor of which, I believe,
is now conceded to him? Now, O! muse, that didst inspire
Homer to describe Achilles' pursuit of Hector, three times
round the walls of Troy; or thou gentler muse, who didst
breathe thy soft afflatus upon Ovid when he described the
race between Apollo and fair Daphne; or thou Caledonian
muse, who didst preside over Walter Scott, when he sung the
race of Fitz James after Murdock of Alpine, or over Robert
Burns, when he made immortal the flight of Tam o' Shanter
from the witches,—either of you or all of the nine at once,
assist me to describe the race between President Caldwell
and Sophomore Faulkner, on the night of the — day of —,
18—. The President lived at that time where his successor
now lives, and was returning about bed time " from walking
up and down upon the earth,"* to see if any of the students
were —— where they ought not to be. As he was mounting
the style which stood where Dr. Wheat's south-east corner
now stands, he spied two young men, busily engaged in
building a fence from that corner across the street to the op-
posite corner. This, by the way, was always the difficulty in
carrying out the manual labor system in our schools, and
constituted the grand distinction between negro-labor and
student-labor : that the negro fenced in the field and hoed up
the weeds; the student hoed up the cotton and fenced in the
street. The lads had just before his appearance heard that
portentous snapping of the ankles, which was a remarkable

---

* Should any of my more serious readers complain of an impropriety in this quota-
tation from Job 1 : vii., they will perhaps find an apology for the allusion in the fact,
well known to all alumni of that period, that *Diabolus* shortened into *Bolus*, was the
common nickname of the President, and that while engaged in their deeds of darkness, they would just as willingly have seen the one as the other.

peculiarity of Dr. Caldwell's locomotives, and was very useful to the evil-doers in enabling them to get several yards the start in the race. As soon as they heard this premonitory crepitation (which, I suppose, they were wont to consider as a providential forewarning of danger, like the rattle of the rattle-snake) one of the fencemakers, whose *nom de guerre* was *Dog*, skulked into a corner and was passed by. Faulkner sprang forward. But I forgot that Homer always spends a line or two in describing his heroes, before he brings them into action. So I must suspend the race, till I have given my audience some idea of Faulkner's person and character. He was a tall, bony, gaunt and grim looking fellow, with shaggy threatening eyebrow—had been at Norfolk during the war of 1813–'14, as a soldier or officer, and had contracted a soldier's love of adventure and frolic, and like Macbeth, would have run from nothing born of mortal, if he had been engaged in a good cause. But building a fence across the street at night, his conscience set down as a deed of darkness, and therefore proved like the conscience of one of the murderers of the Duke of Clarence in Shakspeare's Richard III. "This thing conscience," says he, "is a blushing, shame-faced spirit, that mutinies in a man's bosom; it fills one full of obstacles. A man cannot steal but it accuseth him; a man cannot swear but it checks him. It made me once restore a purse of gold that by chance I found. It beggars any man that keeps it. I'll not meddle with it. It is a dangerous thing. It makes a man a coward." So it proved with the soldier of Norfolk on that memorable night. His conscience made him a coward, but perhaps it enabled him to run the faster, on that occasion, and he might have escaped, had any but "the swift-footed Achilles" given chase. But fate had doomed him to lose this race:

> Forth at full speed the fence-man flew—
> Faulkner of Norfolk, prove thy speed,
> For ne'er had sophmore such need;
> With heart of fire and foot of wind,
> The fierce avenger is behind;
> Fate judges of the rapid strife,

The forfeit death, the prize is life,
He leaves the gates, he leaves the walk behind
Achilles follows like the winged wind;
Thus at the panting dove a falcon flies,
(The swiftest racer of the liquid skies;)
Just when he holds or thinks he holds his prey,
Obliquely wheeling through the aerial way,
With open beak and shrilling cries he springs,
And aims his claws and shoots upon his wings,
Just so around and round the chase they held
One urged by fury, one by fear impelled;
Thus step by step where'er the Trojan wheeled
There swift Achilles compassed round the field;
So on the laboring heroes pant and strain,
While that but flees and this pursues in vain;
Thus three times round the Trojan walls they fly,
The gazing gods lean forward from the sky,
Jove lifts the golden balances that show,
The fates of mortal man and things below;
Here each contending hero's lot he tries
And weighs with equal hand their destinies.
Low sinks the scale surcharged with Faulkner's fate—
Thus heaven's high powers the strife did arbitrate:
Just then the Faulkner tripped, and prostrate fell,
And on the sprawling body pitched—— Caldwell!

Having thus disposed of one of the fencemakers, the victorious President went back in quest of the other, who, instead of coming to the assistance of his friend, had lost no time in leaving the field of action. The President, after beating the bush awhile, returned to the college, where, in the meantime, Faulkner, with clipped wings and fallen crest, had gathered a party in one of the rooms, and was telling the fortunes of the night. Little did he dream that his exulting conqueror was standing close by, in the dark, listening to every word. "And what became of Dog?" inquired one of the party. "Oh! Dog, he took to the woods and I dare say he is running yet." When the court met, the next day, to try the delinquents, it appeared in evidence from the tutor, that *Dog* was the *sobriquet* of Junius Moore. He was accordingly startled by a summons served upon him by old

Daniel Bradley, the college constable, to appear before the faculty as *particeps criminis* with Faulkner. They were both charged with what the lawyers might call tortiously doing a tortuous act. In plainer language, with feloniously, wickedly, and with malice aforethought, then and there. laying down, making, building and constructing, a Virginia fence across the street, against the peace and dignity of the State. Gentlemen, you who have read Cicero's graphic description of the confusion of face and dumbfoundedness of Cataline's accomplices when the consul confronted them with all the damning evidences of their guilt, you can conceive and none but you, the looks and behaviour of the two fencemakers, when Dog was thus unexpectedly arraigned at the bar. "They were so amazed and stupified," says Cicero, " they so looked upon the ground, they so cast furtive glances at each other, that now they seemed to be no longer informed on by others, but to inform on themselves." What the faculty did with the offenders I do not recollect, but remember, young gentlemen, it is all upon the faculty-book, and I hope none of you are ambitions of a place in that chapter of the history of the University or to be enrolled in the Newgate calendar.

As for *Dog*, he deserved a better name, for he was a native-born poet, and he and Philip Alston (a graduate of 1829,) are among the few of our alumni on whose birth Melpomene did smile. Had Moore lived he might have written something to justify these praises. Alston lived long enough to leave some memorials of his genius, but, alas! not long enough for our fame or for his own.

> " For Lycidas is dead, dead ere his prime—
> Young Lycidas—and hath not left his peer !"

That night was one of the *Noctes Atticæ* or *Ambrosianæ*, if you choose so to name them, which signalized the early history of this college. Dr. Caldwell was a good man and a wise man; but I wonder he did not see, that the olympic games of Greece had not a greater attraction for that sprightly people, than such night adventures have for some freshmen—sophomores—juniors—shall I go on? and that for the chance of such a race as this, many a wild collegian would run all the risk of suspension, three nights of every week.

And here, perhaps, it will not be offensive to introduce, among my reminiscences, the *shadow* of a reminiscence, which rests like a *penumbra* among the more distinct impressions on the tablet of my memory. It relates to a man who has long borne a conspicuous and honorable part among the editors of our country—one of the surviving Titans, who has planted his battery not five miles from the throne of Jove, and hurled many a thirty-two pounder at the whitehouse and at the capitol. Should this page chance to meet his eye, and should he recognize in it a faint nucleus of fact, he will laugh at a college legend which always hands down a much better story than it received. President Caldwell once caught some boys in mischief; among the rest he descried one on the top of the college, fastening a *goose* to the very ridge of the roof. "Ah! Joseph, Joseph," said he "I suppose thou art fixing up that poor bird there, as an emblem of thyself." Perhaps that severe cut from his teacher may have goaded the youthful truant to throw away the *goose* forever afterwards, reserving only a quill wherewith to write himself into renown. I hope he will forgive me for thus heralding *his exploits upon the house-tops.*

The bell, too, that everlasting mischief-maker, could never be confined to its legitimate utterances, as long as its notes, at dead of night, set all the faculty on the "*qui vive,*" and when a string, passing from it to some upper window, enabled a freshman, to whom it was a novelty, to create mysterious music, as if gotten up by the spirits of the air. But since the faculty have put it upon the ground that sometimes little boys come here just after their mothers have taken the rattles from about their necks and that they must be amused awhile with some noise, as a substitute, the officers indulge such in bell-ringing until they have got their fill, and then the nuisance is abated.

As for myself, being brought up in the Caldwellian school, I once did try my hand at a night adventure, and sallied forth to catch a party of revellers in the woods. I came upon them by surprise and captured several, but in pursuing one, I got hung in a grape vine, which cured me of pursuing students at night.

There was one other adventure, however, in which *pars magna fui*. As it is characteristic of the times, I will beg pardon for relating it. The two societies, as I have already intimated, were then often at dagger's points with each other, and were sometimes in danger of a general engagement. Like all young things, they easily got angry, and had no objections to a fight, while older animals grow wiser, and find peace much more comfortable and much more dignified than war. (I beg pardon of the august crowned heads that are now butting each other on the plains of Italy*.) On one occasion the champions of the respective bodies came into collision and had a desperate fight, in which one of them, much more of a bully than the other, got his antagonist down and beat him most dreadfully, though I never heard that he *gouged* him. It was a kind of *melee*, several being engaged on both sides. Dr. Caldwell thought it absolutely necessary to adopt vigorous measures to put a stop to such outrages. It appeared that the bully had provoked the fight, and was most to blame. So a writ was taken out to arrest him and carry him to Hillsboro', where the superior court was then sitting. The President's *posse comitatus* was summoned to take him. The house where he secreted himself was surrounded, the besieged leaped out upon the shed, and attempted to jump down; but being headed on all sides, he surrendered at discretion. *I* was one of the guard to Hillsboro'. It was a rainy night, the prisoner purposely kept his horse in a walk, that we might not bring him into town at

---

* That old commentator on the Bible, Matthew Henry, as full of wit as of wisdom, remarks that the prophets very fitly represent the great conquerors of the earth, under the emblems of lions, leopards, bears, rams, he-goats, &c. If so, our allusion in the text is not inapposite, and the world need not care much which has the hardest head, the ram or the he-goat.

night, as a guarded criminal. So we rode up at breakfast time, like a party of travelers, to the hotel, where the judge, and prosecuting officer, and a crowd of people were standing. Our *mittimus* was examined, when lo and behold! the justice of the peace who issued it, had, either accidentally or on purpose, left out of the writ the initials of his office " J. P.," and without those magic letters, it was as harmless as a lion with his head cut off. So the whole proceeding was quashed, the prisoner discharged, the expedition covered with ridicule, and the escort went home pretty well sick of sheriff's business. I beg you, gentlemen in authority here, if you ever have a like occasion, remember the letters J. P.

While we are passing over certain early incidents of Dr. Caldwell's administration, before I leave the subject, the audience will no doubt indulge me in here introducing a brief notice of one of his most valued colleagues and coadjutors, the late lamented Dr. Mitchell. Here let us pause to drop a tear to the memory of this martyr of science. He fell a victim to too great *self-reliance*. This trait in his character, owing, no doubt, in a considerable degree to constitutional temperament, was stimulated and confirmed by a New-England education, in which youth are seldom indulged in that life of ease and indolence so common and so pernicious among ourselves; but are early thrown upon their own enterprize, and invention, and industry, for providing their future livelihood. This characteristic of that part of our country, is remarkably calculated to develop all the latent energies within a youth, whether for good or for evil—a stern necessity " to do or die "—to swim or sink, which may produce a Franklin and a Webster, or peradventure a Benedict Arnold—like the fierce sun of the tropics, which concocts at once the aromatic gums and the deadly poisons.

This self-reliance of our regretted friend, was conspicuous from his first appearance among us. It carried him as a botanist, over almost every hill and meadow and into every nook and corner of our extensive State, alone, and through all weathers; and led him, as a geologist, to scale every mountain and penetrate every cavern, where nature might promise spoils to philosophic curiosity. While youth remained, he escaped unharmed from the perils into which his adventurous spirit pushed him; but, like Milo, the famous athlete of Crotono, he forgot that he was growing old, and was lured to his death by too great confidence in that strength and activity on which he had so often relied with safety. At his age and with his high position as a savant, he was entitled to an escort. He ought not to have been seen venturing alone and unassisted among precipitous cliffs, to make good North-Carolina's claim to the Chimborazo of the Alleganies. He ought to have had a retinue of enthusiastic pupils at his heels, (*magna comitante caterva,*) carrying his chain and his compass, and his barometer, and his tent and traveling chest. And I have no doubt he might have enlisted such a corps of his pupils had he desired and requested it. But his self-reliance seemed to scorn all help, as a confession of incapacity and dependance. A bivouac in a mountain gorge, alone and far from the haunts of men, had something in it inviting to his bold and inquisitive genius. I think I have heard him say, that in one of his visits to the same mountainous region, he had been drenched to the skin by a thunder-storm, and had laid down and slept in his wet clothes, till the morning. That such a man would fall prematurely by his excessive spirit of adventure, was naturally to have been apprehended, and we might have justly cautioned him, in the language of Andromache:

"Too daring man, ah! whither wouldst thou run,
Ah! too forgetful of thy wife and son ;
For sure such courage length of life denies,
And thou *must fall*, thy virtue's sacrifice!"

I have such an opinion of my late friend's undaunted spirit of adventure, that I believe, if he had been one of the scientific corps who accompanied Napoleon in his expedition to Egypt, and if that general had summoned them all before him and said : "I want a man who will go to the biggest of the pyramids, find its secret entrance, explore, lamp in hand, its dark winding galleries, search its inmost penetralia and bring out, if to be found, the sarcophagus of *Cheops* himself"—I believe that Elisha Mitchell would have stept forth and said : " I'll try it." He would have been the very man to have joined Dr. Kane in his Arctic expedition. That daring navigator pushed his investigations to latitude 82° 30', the farthest hyperborian point ever reached by the foot of science, and laid down the coast to within less than 8° of the pole. But if Mitchell had been along with him and Dr. Kane had detached him on an exploring trip, I should not have wondered if the pole itself had been discovered, and Mitchell had tied his boat to the axis of the earth ! Shade of my departed companion ! forgive this sportive ebullition, to which I have been tempted by the recollection of thine own jocose temper and playful spirit. How often, when I have gone to thee, gloomy and fretted by some transient irritation, has thy contagious hilarity and sunshiny face dispelled the cloud from my brow and the spleen from my temper, and I felt the truth of that inspired sentiment: " As iron sharpeneth iron, so does a man sharpen the countenance of his friend." Of such a man might be said, in the beautiful language of Dr. Johnson, that " his death has eclipsed the gaiety of his country and impoverished the general stock of harmless pleasure," as well as of valuable science.

But, brothers of the alumni, I could not excuse myself, and I should but ill perform the duty committed to me this day, if I devoted the whole of this address to amusing or mournful reminiscences of the past. I wish to say something before I sit down, which will be profitable for the future. It may be allowable, on a joyous anniversary like the present, to entertain ourselves and our audience, with some pictures of college life, half a century ago. But it becomes us as educated men, who have gone through the perils and who have reaped the fruits of a collegiate career, to direct our thoughts to the great question how these perils may be encountered and these advantages secured with the least admixture of evil. As lovers of our common country—as North-Carolinians, ambitious of the honor of our State—as men bound to feel for those many parents who trust to these walls their dearest treasure—their sons, that are to bless or to blast their homesteads,—we ought to make it a subject of anxious thought, how to prevent a great college from being a great calamity. As men of reflection and humanity, we must have been often saddened by observing the vast amount of *waste* in human life, human talent and human happiness, which the spectacle of our colleges presents. That there is a strong tendency, when large numbers of young men are congregated together, and live to themselves, with very little intermixture with general society, to become dissipated, riotous and lawless, the history of all colleges proves, both in this country and in Europe. The two universities of England have been long famous as the abodes of licentiousness of all kinds. Mr. Griscom, one of the most respectable and intelligent citizens of New York, visited Oxford about forty years ago, and after witnessing a digraceful scene enacted by a party of students at the hotel* makes the following reflections: " Alas! for such an education as this. What can Latin and Greek and all the store of learning and science have to make amends in an hour of retribution, for a depraved heart and an understanding debased by such vicious indulgence. I cannot but cherish the hope that this incident does not furnish a fair specimen of the morals of the students. It will doubtless happen, that in so large a number as that here collected, in the various colleges, many will bring with them habits extremely unfavorable to morality and subordination. But from the information derived from my guide, who was a

---

* " Of the morality of some of the collegians, I had a most unfavorable specimen. Four or five of them came in the evening, to the inn where I had taken up my quarters, in the principal street in the town. They entered the coffee room, where two or three travelers and myself were sitting, engaged in conversation. After surveying us and the room for some time, they went out but shortly after returned, seated themselves in one of the recesses into which one side of the room is divided, and ordered supper and drink. Their conversation soon assumed a very free cast, and eventually took such a latitude as, I should suppose, would set all Billingsgate at defiance. They abused the waiter, broke a number of things, tore the curtains that enclose the recesses—staid till near twelve o'clock, and then went off, thoroughly soaked with wine, brandy and hot toddy. I was told, the next morning, that two of them were *noblemen*." (A very different thing from NOBLE MEN.)—*Griscom's Year in Europe*, vol. 1 : pp. 60, 61.

moderate man, and certainly well informed with respect to
the habits of the place, and from the observations which
forced themselves upon me in my walks through the streets
and gardens, this evening, I am obliged to deduce the lamentable conclusion that the *morals* of the nation are not much
benefitted by the direct influence of this splendid seat of
learning." And although he inclines to the opinion, that the
state of morals is not quite so bad at Cambridge, yet he
admits it to be a doubtful question, and that this is only a
surmise of his own, and says: "It would be a curious and
interesting subject of inquiry to ascertain, with as much
accuracy as possible, the comparative morality of Oxford
and Cambridge, as it is admitted that in Oxford the collegiate
studies are directed with paramount assiduity to moral philosophy and the higher range of classical learning, while in
Cambridge, mathematics and natural philosophy have a tran-
scendent influence."*

What license, what scorn, what blasphemy, what atheism,
must the rowdies of Cambridge feel at liberty to indulge in,
when they see the disbanded debauchees of the camp suddenly turned into pastors, having the care of souls!

This testimony relates to the state of things at those celebrated universities forty years ago. Have things improved
there since that date? Let us hear the testimony of Sydney
Smith, one of the most distinguished literati of the present
century, whom none will suspect of too austere and puritan-
ical a view of the subject. In a letter written but a few
years ago, to one of his female correspondents, he says: " I

---

* There is one feature which Mr. Griscom observed at his visit to Cambridge,
which is certainly significant, and ominous of a low state of morals. "Since the late
peace," says he, [this was written in 1819, soon after the anti-Napolean armies had
been disbanded,] "a great number of persons, from the army and navy, have entered
as students of divinity, relying on family influence for promotion, and in consequence
of such influence, no inconsiderable number have been promoted, and over the heads,
too, of others, who have devoted many years to the duties of the university. Surely
no wound can be inflicted on religion more deep and deadly than to place a man by
the mere *dictum* of hierarchical authority, in the station of a Christian minister, who
is just reeking from the camp, and who has no qualifications either of head or heart
for the solemn office, and probably no taste for any of its accompaniments except for
the loaves and fishes."—*Vol. 2 : p.* 210.

feel for Mrs. —— about her son at Oxford, knowing as I do. that the only consequences of a university education are the growth of vice and the waste of money."*

In the German universities so far as reports have been published among us, the state of morals is even worse, the frequent practice of duelling being added to the usual vices of college life.

To come nearer home, what has been the experience of our neighboring sister South-Carolina? In the beginning of this century, she began to awaken to the duty and the policy of providing means for the home education of her sons, who had hitherto been educated in the Northern States or in Europe. Somewhat later than we, she created a State college, and endowed it with that enlightened liberality worthy of the intelligence and opulence of her leading men. But, alas! the history of that college proves how useless it is to make all these munificent preparations of faculty, of library, of apparatus and of buildings, if there are not materials enough of the right kind out of which to make students—if the young men of the country are reared up in ease, idleness and luxury, and know that they are rich enough to do without an education. What is the usual course with such young men? They go to college; they there find numbers of idlers like themselves, they find study irksome and disgusting, pleasure spreads out her seductions before them, they are indulged with plenty of money, and habits of ruinous dissipation follow as the necessary results. If they are sent home, what penalty there awaits them? A horse, a gun and dog, fine clothes and the ladies! Who would immure himself in a college cell with such companions as Thucydides and his crabbed Greek, or Loomis's Differential and Integral Calculus, when by going down street and "getting up a row," he can be sent home to so much pleasanter employment and company? The result of South-Carolina's experiment upon a college, we have from authority the most unsuspicious and authentic. One of the most respectable alumni, one of the

---

* Life, vol 2: p. 402.

oldest judges on the bench of that State has given his testimony, which has been copied into most of the newspapers of the land. "I have known that institution," says Judge O'Neall, "intimately since 1811, when I first entered its walls, and I have no hesitation in saying that one-fourth of its students have been affected injuriously or destroyed by intoxicating drinks. Indeed I fully believe that one-fourth of its graduates sleep in drunkards' graves." He goes on to say, however, that "notwithstanding this dread scourge. South-Carolina college has accomplished an immense amount of good," &c. A valuable lesson was learned from the results of the Cooper administration of that institution. Dr. Thomas Cooper was called to the presidency from his high reputation as a man of science and general learning, and perhaps with some reference to his orthodoxy on political questions, then deeply agitating that State. It would have been hard to find a man of more multifarious learning. He was a lawyer, a statesman, a physician, a philosopher, natural and moral, and somewhat even of a theologian ; but withal he was an infidel, an atheist. And the college soon took the type of its head. Infidelity and irreligion took possession of the seat and centre of knowledge, and therefore soon became rife through the State. A State college is the eye of the body politic, and "if the eye be evil the whole body shall be full of darkness." The college was broken down by dissipation and disorder ; parents lost all confidence, and durst not expose their sons to the double danger of infidel principles and profligate example. At length Gov. McDuffie in his message to the legislature, was obliged to report the State college as a failure ; and though an infidel himself, he candidly admitted that the prevalence of infidel sentiments had destroyed the public confidence and reduced the college to its present low condition, and he therefore advised a re-organization of the faculty and a new trial for success under different auspices. Accordingly three of the foremost men in the State for talents and religious character, were installed as president and professors, and a special professorship was created of *Christian Evidences*. Very soon the college regained its former patronage, religion was respected, the gospel powerfully·preached twice every Sunday in the college chapel, and infidelity, formerly triumphant and open-mouthed, was now silent and humbled, if not extinct. Here was an experiment whose fruits I trust will be permanently and extensively useful, namely : that a literary institution, without the religious element to leaven the mass, will not be supported by the people of this country.

The University of Virginia had to go through the same experience. It was the child of Mr. Jefferson, whose infidelity was well known. and had a contagious influence on the leading public men of the State. No provision was made for any religious worship or religious instruction in the university. The institution, for several of the first years of its existence, had a bad name for vice and irreligion—the religious public mourned and complained that the State university founded and supported by the votes and the treasure of the commonwealth, for the education of the sons of the commonwealth, should ignore christianity, and be given up to anti-christian influences. This was the *apparent* design, by leaving out religion entirely in the course of instruction and in the appointment of officers. To do Mr. Jefferson justice. this seems not to have been in his contemplation. Unbeliever as he was, himself, he was too shrewd a politician, and too well acquainted with the people of this country, to attempt a literary establishment among us, having none of the moral and popular influences of christianity. His idea was this, as I learned from his own lips, when I paid a visit to Monticello, in 1823, only three years before his death, and but a short time before the university went into operation. He thought·that the established American principle of non-interference in religious matters, and the division of our people into different sects, rendered it improper and impracticable to incorporate in the plan of the university any provision for the teaching of religion. But it was announced publicly, that all the religious bodies were authorized and were encouraged to establish, at the seat of the university, any foundations and lectureships that they might deem expedient, and they were promised the free use of the library and of the lectures of the academical department. This seems to vindicate Mr. Jefferson on this point. But, as the suggestion above mentioned was not adopted by the various religious denominations, after a few years' experiment, the absence of christianity was proved to be a serious evil, and disreputable to the university. So the faculty and students by common consent, determined to call a chaplain to perform the ordinary religious services, and that they might obviate the jealousy of religious sects, the chaplain was to be chosen from the prevalent religious bodies, in rotation. This, I believe, has worked well, and to the satisfaction of all. The present arrangements also give to all ministers and candidates for the ministry, the privilege of attending gratuitously the lectures of the professors, which, it would seem, ought to appease all alarms and silence all complaints.

The college of which we boast ourselves to be sons, was founded in an era most dark and inauspicious to religion — the close of the last and the beginning of the present century. Our country had just emerged from a long, distressing war, and it is well known that war has a hardening effect upon the minds of men, familiarizing them with blood and death, and rendering them skeptical and indifferent in matters relating to a future world. To this add the overshadowing influence of France. The splendor of her philosophers and political economists had then attracted the admiration of the world; her powerful fellowship in arms had helped us happily through our struggle for liberty, and then her imitation of us in bursting her own shackles,—all these ties had bound us to her destines with an enthusiasm and self-sacrifice which had well nigh engulphed us in the same devouring whirlpool that finally swallowed up her first republic. She reciprocated all our enthusiasm, and received our Franklin in Paris with the honors of a demigod, condensing into one pregnant Latin hexameter his two greatest exploits—the snatching of lightning from heaven, and the sceptre from tyrants:

" Eripuit cœlo fulmen, sceptrum que tyrannis."*

* Turgot, the famous political economist, was the author of this beautiful eulogium.

Unhappily when France overturned the throne and the Bastile, she overturned, with the same convulsive throes, the temple of God, and set up as her only object of worship, the goddess Liberty—liberty not only from the chains of despots, but from all belief in future responsibility. This portentous atheism spread its disastrous influence over most of our public men, and hence the works of Voltaire and his royal patron, Frederick of Prussia, of Rousseau, Helvetius, Bolingbroke, Hume, Gibbon and Paine, were found in the libraries of our principal families, however small these libraries were. Some of these, presented by trustees and others, were among the most conspicuous books in our university and society libraries, in their early beginnings. As the *cock* was the national emblem of France, it is hardly vulgar to quote here our homely proverb: " As the old cock crows the young one learns." Our first professors and students caught the Gallic infection; and Dr. Caldwell among his earliest difficulties, had to struggle with infidelity in the faculty and infidelity among the students; and hence, among his sermons of that date, many will be found in refutation of objections against christianity. The same difficulties Dr. Dwight was contending with at Yale college, to the presidency of which he was called a few years before this date. From the commencement of Dr. Caldwell's administration the christian religion has been recognised and taught in this institution, and its laws have required the students to attend such religious services as they were called to by the professors. Since that time the growth of the several ecclesiastical bodies, has made it right and important to consult their wishes by representation in the academic corps; and it would seem that the best practicable plan has been fallen on to allay sectarian jealousy, and to give christianity such prominence in our collegiate system, as to impress our undergraduates with the conviction that it is venerated as of divine origin, and as the religion of our country.

But after all this public provision for the maintenance of religious influence and of moral habits, it is a lamentable fact that colleges will nourish within their bosom, a large amount of vicious dissipation, idleness and profusion. The two great obstacles to government and incentives to disorder are the congregation of large numbers of youth into houses by themselves, and the use of intoxicating drinks. Whether we have not made a mistake in thus isolating the students from family society, and crowding them together in such numbers under one roof, may admit of painful doubt. Judge O'Neall, whom I quoted a little while ago, gives it as his decided conviction, that dormitories ought to be done away with, and the students distributed among respectable families. Dr. James W. Alexander, of New York. one of the first men of this country, an alumnus of Princeton, and for a long time a professor there, in a letter received from him a few years since, says: "Of all absurd things in the world, one of the most absurd is to put a great number of boys together, in a large building, to keep house by themselves." This is the first difficulty, but whether the plan proposed as a remedy would succeed better has not, I believe, been put to the test. We cannot therefore say of the recipe: *probatum est.* The other difficulty, the use of intoxicating liquors, is the gigantic evil of colleges, and leads all reflecting persons, as well as Mr. Griscom, sometimes to doubt whether all the benefits of public education are not outweighed by this enormous mischief to the morals and happiness of our families. War is, while it lasts, perhaps the most terrific calamity with which our race is scourged. Pestilence too, now and then, poisons the common element we all do breathe, and more than decimates our cities. These evils, however, are intermittent. They leave long intervals of repose and healthful enjoyment. But intemperance, begun in youth and often continued and aggravated through tedious years of shame and sorrow, in so many families—this, this, is the running ulcer of our social body; this is the perennial, fetid, stygian flood, that is circling round and round the land, and pouring its poisonous tide into our sacred homes. This it is which causes more human hearts to ache and more human faces to blush than any other cause. In vain have been all your temperance societies. In vain your temperance lecturers have been sent through the length of the land—gifted with tragic powers to make the public weep over the horrors of drunkenness, and with comic powers to make the drunkard the laughing stock of the world. In vain have been all these schemes to abate the nuisance. Intemperance has grown under all these appliances, like the cancer spreading under the surgeon's knife, or the Hydra multiplying its heads under the club of Hercules.

> Alas! Leviathan is not thus tamed;
> Laughed at he laughs again, and stricken hard,
> Turns to the stroke his adamantine scales,
> That fear no discipline from human hands.

And if this disease is so pernicious in its sporadic form, turning a home here and a home there into a habitation of wretchedness, what must it be when concentrated in a public institution, a multitude countenancing and stimulating each other, "despising the shame," and by their united strength breaking down every barrier! A college thus tainted is like our great western river, with all its swollen affluents, bursting all the embankments, and carrying terror, and devastation, and malaria over the fruitful valley which it ought to adorn and fertilize. For this single vice is at the root of all collegiate disturbances and delinquencies. Of every drinking student may be said what was said of Judas Iscariot: " With the *sop* Satan entered into him." Hence all the counsels of educators, all the ingenuity of physicians, all the discoveries of chemistry, all the wisdom and power of legislative bodies, should be put in requisition to contend with this portentous mischief. And he who shall discover a cure or even an alleviation of this curse of humanity, will deserve a monument higher and more enduring than the pyramids, and be entitled to a gratitude deeper and wider than that accorded to Dr. Jenner, who has relieved the world of the terrors of small pox. Premiums are offered for all improvements in the industrial and economical arts, and for the best essays on all moral subjects; but the richest premium will he deserve, who, by some chymic art, shall make young colle-

gians loathe intoxicating drinks, or by some happy improve-
ment in political economy, shall drive ardent spirits out of
the land as an article of manufacture or of commerce. The
might of *man* has failed; may we not appeal to the softer
but more potent influence of *woman?* Will not the ladies,
themselves safe and superior to this infirmity, come to the
rescue of our powerless sex? *We* are called the stronger
sex and they the weaker; but as to temptations to vice they
are the stronger and we are the weaker sex. I have the
same opinion of them that Lord Chatham had of the English
soldiers: "They can achieve anything but impossibilities."*
They are not good at making large bargains, I admit, as is
proved by the price they have agreed to give for Mt. Ver-
non; but even there, the bargain is to their credit, showing
that they estimate the "value received," not in the worth of
the land, but in the testimony of national gratitude and in
sending an embassador around the land to teach in honied
accents, the grandest lesson this family of matrons can learn,
namely: by loving their common father, to love and cherish
the united republic which he lived and labored and suffered
to establish. Let those who have entered with so much zeal
into this national "labor of love" now join their hearts in
another, touching more nearly the happiness of their country
and of the world. Let them proclaim with their sovereign
voice, from one end of the continent to the other, that their
smiles and their hands are the prize of *sobriety* alone. From
all their lips let there be heard the general chorus:

> Young men, young men who love your drink,
> Your bark of hope and bliss must sink;
> We'll never trust with you our life—
> You cannot, shall not have a wife.

I venture with diffidence to make the following suggestions. It seems hopeless to put a stop to the use of all stimulating drinks. All nations have used them, and God consti-

---

* The French have a proverb that truly expresses the power of woman: "Les
femmes pouvent tout, parcequ'elles gouvernent les personnes qui gouvernent tout."

tuted wine with corn as a part of his special gifts to his people, in the Holy Land. Thus the inspired writer says: "He causeth the grass to grow for the cattle and herb for the service of man, and wine that maketh glad the heart of man, and oil to make his face to shine, and bread which strengtheneth man's heart." Here you find wine mentioned like grass and herb, and oil, and bread, as gifts equally expressive of the kindness of Heaven. What God gives as a tonic and stimulant, along with the nutriment of man, cannot, if soberly and prudently used, be hurtful either to body or mind. In conformity with these providential bestowments of the old dispensation, we find the Saviour, in the New Testament, using wine at his meals, though it exposed him to the slander of being a wine-bibber—turning water into wine for the use of the guests, at a marriage banquet, and appointing wine to be used at his own sacred supper. Now I by no means intend it to be understood that because in that day and country the fermented juice of the grape was a native product and a licensed beverage, therefore the adulterous and poisonous mixtures in use among us are lawful and expedient; nor would I be understood as saying that the banishment of even *pure wine* would be beyond the right and duty of college authorities, any more than it would be beyond their right to prohibit a certain kind of *food*, if it was found that that kind of food led generally to gluttony and sickness. Besides, in modern times so many other beverages have been introduced, less dangerous and perhaps more nutritious, that we have less reason to use the wine of the shops, which is anything else but the juice of the grape. But what I am now aiming at is this: to inquire whether we could not, by introducing the vine among our agricultural products, make within ourselves a domestic beverage, safe and pleasant, and drive out the pestiferous liquors, foreign and homemade, which are now the bane of our land. An enlightened foreigner from Germany, Mr. Schweinitz, who was honored with a seat in the board of trustees, and who used sometimes, to visit this place, declared that this locality where we now are, was the very country for the grape and the manufacture of wine. Why should not our enlightened and more wealthy farmers, who can afford to make the experiment, instead of forever moving round in the same circle of crops, (corn, wheat, cotton, tobacco,) venture upon the culture of the grape and an experiment in wine, at first on a small scale?* If our country should be found capable of producing light wines, harmless as a common drink, it might have a greater effect in promoting temperance than the effort at total abstinence. It is admitted that the people of France are in general temperate, though the use of wine is universal, and that it is a rare thing to see a drunken man in that country. Mr. Hentz, formerly professor of French in this college, who spent his early life in Paris, used to say that he never saw a drunken man till he was seventeen years of age, and that he was at a loss to account for the singularity of his behaviour, ascribing it to a derangement. This superior sobriety of that light, and giddy, and impetuous nation, cannot be attributed to any *moral* cause, and is probably due to the fact that a cheap and innocuous beverage is accessible to every body. In the absence of wine from our country, might not some other innocent liquors be brought into use—beer, mead, cider, raspberry wine, &c.? At Princeton, when I was there in 1813, malt beer was a part of the college dinner; and in Yale college, it was allowed as a perquisite to an indigent student, to sell liquors of that kind to the students; whether it was abandoned at both of those great institutions, as leading to injurious consequences, I never heard. I throw out these suggestions with some apprehension lest a bad use may be made of them, but the disease is so desperate it warrants bold experiments. From long thought and experience and from the high authorities I have quoted, I have been led to form the theory of a college, of which if my audience will

---

* I annex the following recent document on this subject:

Wine in Ohio.—An experienced writer who has one of the best vineyards in Hamilton county, says that four hundred gallons of wine per acre may be safely depended upon this year, as the product of the grape crop. The fermented juice of the grape readily commands, when new, an average of $1 25 per gallon. At the above rate the crop will yield $500 per acre—about the most profitable crop that is produced in this country.

have patience with me I will give them a brief outline. It is impracticable, to be sure, in an old country, and where all the expenditures of buildings have been already incurred. But I cannot help desiring to avail myself of so large an audience to present my thoughts on this subject for the consideration of an enlightened public. The generous donations by Congress of extensive lands for educational purposes in our new States, would have furnished, and in some may yet furnish most favorable opportunities and facilities for carrying such a plan into execution : Let a tract of one or more square miles, healthy and beautiful in its aspect, and having an abundance of fine water, be selected as the location. Let this territory remain, *in perpetuum*, the property of the trustees; let not a foot of it be sold. Let a village be laid out in convenient lots, and let respectable families be invited to *lease* them, for a term of years, and put up suitable houses, obligating themselves to take a certain number of boarders, and to keep no intoxicating drinks, under penalty of ejectment. This would give the trustees a control over the population, and enable them to exclude all improper inhabitants. The only public buildings then required would be houses for professors and public rooms for lectures, library and apparatus; and the large sums heretofore expended in providing dormitories would be saved for endowing professorships and scholarships, and procuring library and apparatus. This plan would promise to obviate the disturbances incident to a steward's table, the disorders generated by having large numbers in one house, and would if settlers of the right sort could be obtained, promote gentility of manners by intercourse with private families, and in case of sickness secure requisite quiet comfort and attendance.

Such is the theory, and a fair vision it affords; but I am distrustful of all theories, and I should like to know whether there is anywhere an institution on this plan, and how it works. Favorers of things as they are, and conservatives suspicious of innovations, I confess may overcast this fair vision with forebodings of ills still greater than the present. A prophet less hopeful and perhaps more sagacious than I, may descry looming in the dim future visions of landlords with broken heads for informing the faculty that, last night, there was a card and wine party up stairs—visions of enamored students and love-sick daughters in every boarding house; Corydon sighing for Chloe, and Chloe sighing, not for Corydon but for Daphnis—then dark spectres of Corydon and Daphnis in deadly strife—Amyntas

> "Sporting with Amaryllis in the shade,
> Or with the tangles of Neara's hair,"*

instead of with his Demosthenes and Plato,—the scene winding up with five matches on commencement night between so many graduates and so many daughters of their respective landlords. Alas! I should have to insert among the conditions of my Utopian colony that the landlords should have no daughters, or should send them all off to school. These dark possibilities clouding my fairy vision, will, I fear, prevent its ever being realized, and induce the old fogies to fold their arms in scornful tranquility, saying: "All the difference between the old plan and the new one will be, that instead of having one Ætna, with now and then a "great blow-out and have done with it," you will have fifty little smithies, with the roar of the bellows, the clanging of the anvil and the showers of sparks forever annoying you." So we see that on this, as on most subjects, "much may be said on both sides."

After so long an address, can I, ought I to be insensible to the flattering attention and marks of approbation with which it has been received? I well know what has worked so mightily in my favor. Never was speaker more fortunate in the temper of the house. Among the charms which, according to old Homer, Jove conferred upon his darling daughter, Venus, was that of *philommeides;* she was *the queen of smiles, the laughter-loving Aphrodite.* So the presence of the chief magistrate of the Union has made every one joyous—it has given me a *laughter-loving* audience, and among

* Milton's Lycidas.

them many a Venus, with lambent lightnings playing about her eyes, encircled with the irresistible Cestus, and with the little rogue Cupid sitting at her feet ever sharpening his burning arrows on a bloody whetstone.*

And if I owe an apology to my kind and indulgent audience for the parti-colored character of this address, this motley mixture of the serious and the ludicrous, here is my defence: Such is life, in which shade and sunshine chase each other over the plain—in which joy and sorrow rapidly alternate in our hearts—in which smiles often shine through our tears and dry them up—and again tears start forth and extinguish the light of our smiles. Such is life, and such did Shakspeare, the greatest painter of life, represent it. His pictures of man are neither unmixed tragedies nor unmixed comedies, but tragi-comedies. Such alternations seem to be our Creator's design.

> The lights and shades, whose well-accorded strife,
> Give all the strength and color of our life.

Sorrow in advance makes the arrival of gladness more glad, and sorrow apprehended in the future chastises and tempers the transports of present pleasure, and mingles all our rejoicings with salutary trembling.

> Alas! by some degree of wo,
> We every bliss must gain;
> The heart can ne'er a transport know,
> That never knew a pain.

And yet something whispers me that the retrospect I have taken ought to have inspired a more serious strain. Of the long line of alumni with whom I have been contemporary, how few survive!

> Apparent rari mantes in gurgite vasto.

* "Ridet Venus, ferus et Cupido,
Semper ardentes, acuens sagittas,
Cote cruenta." [Bur.

4

Of seven eminent men with whom I have had the honor to co-operate as professor in this institution, six have now passed off from the stage of action. Caldwell, Hentz, Mitchell, Andrews, Anderson and Olmsted are no more. Their accents which once contributed to enlighten and adorn our State, are now hushed in the voiceless grave, and perhaps ere another anniversary revolves around, and brings you together again, the two who yet remain will be gathered with those who have gone before them. To one who looks back fifty or sixty years, what a shadow is man! how fleeting, how trifling do seem all his interests and schemes, his hopes and his fears! The thought extorted a sigh even from a pagan moralist:

"O! curas hominum! O! quantum est in rebus inane."*

How fading the honors of earth, how empty the applause of men! But happy, thrice happy we, that this fading pageant is not all,—that our deathless souls, never satisfied with the limited and transient, and always reaching after something illimitable and infinite, shall, if purified by religion, enter upon a state where all our companions and joys shall be perfect and unchangable:

Where Time, and Pain, and Chance, and Death expire;
Where momentary ages are no more;
Where seraphs gather immortality,
On Life's fair tree, fast by the throne of God.

* Persius.